The Frog Princess

✦ ✦ ✦ ✦ ✦ ✦ ✦ ✦ ✦ ✦ ✦ ✦ ✦ ✦ ✦ ✦ ✦

AUTHOR'S NOTE

There are three hundred variants of the story of the frog bride found
throughout Europe. I have freely told mine from Italian versions, using
as my principal sources *Il principe che sposò una rana* by Italo Calvino,
retold from Domenico Comparetti, 4, Monferrato, Piedmont; and
"The Frog," translated by Mrs. Andrew Lang, *The Violet Fairy Book*.

Text copyright © 1994 by Laura Cecil
Illustrations copyright © 1994 by Emma Chichester Clark

First published in Great Britain in 1994 by Jonathan Cape Limited,
a division of Random House UK Ltd.
First published in the United States in 1995 by Greenwillow Books.

Laura Cecil and Emma Chichester Clark have asserted their right
to be identified as the author and illustrator of this work.

Printed in Hong Kong
First American Edition 10 9 8 7 6 5 4 3 2 1

LIBRARY OF CONGRESS CATALOGING-IN-PUBLICATION DATA
Cecil, Laura.
The frog princess / [adapted] by Laura Cecil; illustrated by
Emma Chichester Clark.
p.   cm.
"First published in Great Britain in 1994
by Jonathan Cape"—T.p. verso.
Summary: Forced to marry an ugly frog, the youngest son of the
queen is astounded to learn that the frog is really a beautiful princess.
ISBN 0-688-13506-4   [1. Fairy tales. 2. Folklore—Russia.]
I. Chichester Clark, Emma, ill.   II. Title.   PZ8.C295Fr   1995
398.24'5278—dc20   [E]   94-4573   CIP   AC

RETOLD BY
LAURA CECIL

The Frog Princess

ILLUSTRATED BY
EMMA CHICHESTER CLARK

GREENWILLOW BOOKS NEW YORK

There once was a queen who had three sons.

The eldest, Prince Bruno,
loved food. He had a different
cook for each meal of the day.

The second son, Prince Lucca,
loved clothes, and he would change
his costume every two hours.

The youngest, Prince Marco, was a dreamer.
He loved to lie in the grass gazing at flowers and insects.

One day the queen said, "Bruno, you spend too much time eating. Lucca, you spend too much time changing your clothes. And Marco, you spend too much time thinking about nothing. It is time you found sensible wives."

"But we don't know how," said the princes.
"Don't worry about that," said the queen, and she gave
them each a bow and arrow. "Shoot your arrow as far
as you can, and where it lands, you will find your bride."

Bruno's arrow landed on
the roof of a baker's shop.
The baker's daughter was
as round and brown as one of
her father's loaves. Bruno thought
she looked good enough to eat.

Lucca's arrow landed in a tailor's
garden. His daughter was as thin
and white as one of her father's
threads. Lucca thought she would
match his new costume perfectly.

But Marco's arrow landed in a ditch, and the
only bride he found was a little green frog.

Bruno and Lucca brought their brides to the palace for everyone to admire. But when the queen asked Marco why he had not brought his bride, he blushed and said, "She can't come because she has a croak in her throat."

"Now," said the queen, "I am tired of ruling this kingdom, and since all my sons are fools, whichever one has found the cleverest wife shall become king.

"I will set your brides three tasks. First, each must bake a perfect loaf of bread." And she handed each prince a bag of flour.

Poor Marco was in despair. How could a frog make a
loaf of bread? He sat down by the ditch where his frog
bride lived. Flop! Out she jumped beside him.
"Oh, little frog," he said, "I don't know what to do.
The queen wants you to bake a perfect loaf of bread."
"Don't fret," said the frog. "I'll see to it."
The next day when Marco returned, the frog handed
him a walnut and said, "Trust me. All will be well."

Prince Bruno and Prince Lucca presented the loaves their
brides had made. The baker's daughter had made an
enormous loaf like a castle. The tailor's daughter
had made a loaf as long and sharp as
a knitting needle.

Marco's brothers laughed when he presented the walnut. But when the queen cracked it open, out grew a delicious loaf shaped like a flower. She ate a mouthful and exclaimed, "This is perfect!"

"The second task is to weave a perfect length of cloth,"
said the queen, and she handed each prince a bag of silk.

Marco went back to his frog bride. Flop! Out she jumped beside him.
"Oh, little frog," he said sadly, "I don't know what to do.
The queen wants you
to weave a perfect
length of cloth."
"Don't fret," said the frog.
"I'll see to it."

The next week when Marco returned, the frog handed him
a golden hazelnut and said, "Trust me. All will be well."

The baker's daughter had woven a cloth as coarse as a flour bag. The tailor's daughter had woven an elaborate tapestry. It was so heavy it took three men to carry it. But when the queen opened Marco's golden hazelnut, out slid cloth so fine that it flowed all over the throne room without stopping. The queen cried out, "Is there no end to it?"

Whereupon the cloth stopped growing and rolled itself into a neat bundle. "Your bride is a clever girl, Marco," said the queen.

"The final task will be to train a dog," said the queen. "Your brides will have one month to do this." And she gave each prince a puppy.

Marco didn't know what to do. He sat mournfully by the ditch. Flop! Out jumped the frog beside him. "Oh, little frog," he said, "this time the queen has set an impossible task. She wants you to train this puppy in one month." "Don't fret," said the frog. "I'll see to it."

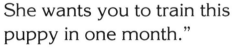

One month later when Marco returned, the frog handed him a tiny silver basket with a lid and said, "Trust me. All will be well."

Everyone had assembled at the palace for the climax of the competition between the three brides. Bruno's bride dragged in her dog. It was enormously fat from eating all the scraps in her father's bakery. It fell over at the queen's feet and began to snore.

Lucca's bride carried her dog. They were wearing matching brocade coats and hats. The dog was extremely thin and elegant, but it was so weak it could hardly walk. Lucca's bride gave it very little to eat in case it grew too fat for its grand clothes.

But when the queen opened Marco's tiny silver basket,
out jumped the most enchanting little dog.

It could count,   march on its hind legs,

and play the guitar.

There was no doubt in the queen's mind who had won. "Marco, bring your bride to court," she said. "She must have lost that croak in her throat by now. The wedding will be tomorrow."

"All is lost," said Marco when he saw the little frog again.
"Three times you have shown me more kindness than any
  friend in the world, but this time not even you can help. The
  queen has commanded that I marry my bride tomorrow."
"Would you take me for your wife?" asked the frog.
"If you will have me," said Marco. He did not want to marry
  a frog, but he could not bear to hurt her feelings.
"Trust me," said the frog. "All will be well."

She vanished into the ditch, but a moment later she returned
sitting on a water lily leaf drawn by two large snails.

Marco set out for the palace with the frog following slowly behind. After a while he looked around, but she was nowhere to be seen. Then, to his horror, he saw a tiny frog skin, a water lily leaf, and two snail shells lying under a tree. At that moment he heard the clip-clop of horses' hooves.

He looked up, and there, driving a carriage,
was the most beautiful girl he had ever seen.
"I am your frog bride," she said. "I was a princess until
a cruel enchanter changed me into a frog. But now
you have said you will marry me, the spell is broken."

When the queen saw the princess, she said, "Marco, why did you hide your bride away? She is as beautiful as she is clever. You have won the kingdom."
So Marco and the princess were crowned king and queen, and there was dancing and feasting for nine days and nine nights.

And for the rest of their days
King Marco and his queen
lived in great joy and happiness.